A Mystery Blossoms!

Mimsy smiled as she disappeared into the crowd. Nancy had never seen her so happy. It was like she'd already won the first-place ribbon.

"Where'd Deirdre and Suzie go?" Bess asked, looking around.

Nancy scanned the Grand Ballroom. She didn't see the girls anywhere. "I'm not sure. Maybe they've discovered the chocolate fountain." Nancy giggled as she walked toward the dessert table. They'd spend the afternoon eating sweets and taking pictures with all the amazing flowers.

Nancy and Bess were reaching for chocolate strawberries when someone screamed. The girls turned around. There, across the room, was Mimsy Bouret. Her face was completely white. She covered her heart with her hand.

"What is it? What happened?" Helene called out from the stage.

Mimsy pointed to an empty vase. "Someone stole my roses!" she yelled. "They're gone!"

Join the CLUE CREW
& solve these other cases!

#1 *Sleepover Sleuths*

#2 *Scream for Ice Cream*

#3 *Pony Problems*

#4 *The Cinderella Ballet Mystery*

#5 *Case of the Sneaky Snowman*

#6 *The Fashion Disaster*

#7 *The Circus Scare*

#8 *Lights, Camera . . . Cats!*

#9 *The Halloween Hoax*

#10 *Ticket Trouble*

#11 *Ski School Sneak*

#12 *Valentine's Day Secret*

#13 *Chick-napped!*

#14 *The Zoo Crew*

#15 *Mall Madness*

#16 *Thanksgiving Thief*

#17 *Wedding Day Disaster*

#18 *Earth Day Escapade*

#19 *April Fool's Day*

#20 *Treasure Trouble*

#21 *Double Take*

#22 *Unicorn Uproar*

#23 *Babysitting Bandit*

#24 *Princess Mix-up Mystery*

#25 *Buggy Breakout*

#26 *Camp Creepy*

#27 *Cat Burglar Caper*

#28 *Time Thief*

#29 *Designed for Disaster*

#30 *Dance off*

#31 *Make-a-Pet Mystery*

#32 *Cape Mermaid Mystery*

#33 *The Pumpkin Patch Puzzle*

#34 *Cupcake Chaos*

#35 *Cooking Camp Disaster*

#36 *The Secret of the Scarecrow*

NANCY DREW

#37 AND THE CLUE CREW®

The Flower Show Fiasco

BY CAROLYN KEENE

ILLUSTRATED BY MACKY PAMINTUAN

Aladdin
New York London Toronto Sydney New Delhi

🐦 ALADDIN

An imprint of Simon & Schuster Children's Publishing Division
1230 Avenue of the Americas, New York, NY 10020
First Aladdin paperback edition March 2014
Text copyright © 2014 by Simon & Schuster, Inc.
Illustrations copyright © 2014 by Macky Pamintuan
All rights reserved, including the right of reproduction in whole or in part in any form.
ALADDIN and related logo, NANCY DREW, and NANCY DREW AND THE CLUE CREW
are registered trademarks of Simon & Schuster, Inc.
For information about special discounts for bulk purchases, please contact
Simon & Schuster Special Sales at 1-866-506-1949 or business@simonandschuster.com.
The Simon & Schuster Speakers Bureau can bring authors to your live event.
For more information or to book an event contact the Simon & Schuster Speakers Bureau
at 1-866-248-3049 or visit our website at www.simonspeakers.com.
Designed by Karina Granda
The text of this book was set in ITC Stone Informal.
Manufactured in the United States of America 0214 OFF
2 4 6 8 10 9 7 5 3 1
Library of Congress Control Number 2013948652
ISBN 978-1-4424-8668-3
ISBN 978-1-4424-8669-0 (eBook)

CONTENTS

CHAPTER ONE: YOU'RE INVITED . . . · · · · · · · · · · · 1

CHAPTER TWO: FRIENDLY COMPETITION · · · · · · · · · 10

CHAPTER THREE: THE MISSING BLOOMS · · · · · · · · · 16

CHAPTER FOUR: TICKTOCK, TICKTOCK · · · · · · · · · 27

CHAPTER FIVE: UNUSUAL SUSPECTS · · · · · · · · · · 32

CHAPTER SIX: HE SAID, SHE SAID · · · · · · · · · · · 41

CHAPTER SEVEN: CAUGHT IN THE ACT · · · · · · · · · 48

CHAPTER EIGHT: THE MYSTERY MAN · · · · · · · · · · 60

CHAPTER NINE: A CONFESSION · · · · · · · · · · · · 69

CHAPTER TEN: THE PERFECT ROSE · · · · · · · · · · 78

Grace Rousseau
12 Massasoit Way
Mattapoisett, MA 02739

ChaPTER ONE

You're Invited . . .

"Race you!" Nancy yelled. She pedaled up the steep hill to her house but was nearly out of breath. Bess and George rode behind her on their bikes, trying to keep up.

George pushed down hard on the pedals, doubling her pace. "And George Fayne is pulling into the lead. . . ." She lowered her voice so she sounded like a sports announcer. Her bike wheel inched in front of Nancy's. "It's a close race here in River Heights. Who will win? It's anyone's guess!"

Bess climbed off her bike. She held on to the handlebars as she walked up the hill. After riding around the neighborhood for an hour, Bess was too tired to race her friends. Instead she played the cheerleader, rooting for best friend Nancy Drew. "Come on, Nancy! Don't give up just yet!"

Nancy pushed as hard as she could. She leaned forward, gripping the handlebars. George and Nancy were neck and neck. As they climbed to the top of the hill, the rest of the neighborhood came into view. The street dead-ended, with just five houses up ahead. Nancy pedaled as fast as she was able to, but George was faster. Just as the road flattened out George pulled ahead. She threw one arm up and hooted.

"I did it! George Fayne is the winner!" She laughed.

Nancy smiled. She'd known her best friends, Bess Marvin and George Fayne, since before they could talk. Bess and George were cousins, and they loved doing everything with Nancy. Together they rode bikes, had sleepovers, and danced around Bess's room to silly songs on the radio. They spent summers swimming and camping, and winter breaks building snow forts. But their favorite thing to do was solve mysteries. Together they formed the Clue Crew. It seemed like they were always finding cases in their hometown of River Heights.

George's fist was still raised high in the air. Seeing how excited she was, Nancy couldn't help but laugh. "You won fair and square," Nancy said. "But tomorrow there'll be a rematch!"

Nancy's house came into view up ahead. George pointed to a blue house with white shutters just a few doors down. "Look! The lights are on. Miss Bouret must be back."

Bess rode up beside them. The girls paused at the picket fence, which was covered in pink blooming flowers. The front door was open and the sprinkler was on. Those seemed like sure signs that Miss Bouret had returned from her two-week-long trip to Paris.

Nancy glanced at the rosebushes that lined the front of the house. Mimsy Bouret, one of Nancy's favorite neighbors, had a garden that looked like it was out of a magazine. There were blooming plants everywhere. Mimsy loved to walk around her garden, teaching Nancy and her friends the names of all the different plants. There were gardenias, lilacs, hydrangeas, and tulips. Her most impressive flowers were her roses, though, which she put Nancy in charge of while she was away. Every afternoon Nancy carefully watered the plants. She always made sure to give them just the right amount. Taking care of Miss Bouret's garden was a big task, and Nancy worried that she might mess it up. But the peach roses still looked perfect.

Just then the front door opened. "Hello, my little darlings!" she cried as she sashayed out of her house. Her red curls were piled on the top of her head and she wore a floral blouse with lace around the collar. The entire four years Nancy had known Miss Bouret, she'd never seen her in anything except flower-print shirts. Sometimes it seemed like everything she owned was covered with tiny roses or blooming lilies, even her socks.

"You're back!" Nancy called out. She set her bike against the fence and stepped inside the yard. It smelled like the Perfume Mania store in the River Heights Mall. "How was Paris?"

"Fabulous!" Miss Bouret shouted. "I shopped and did some sightseeing. The Eiffel Tower, the Louvre Museum. I walked along the River Seine and I ate about ten pounds' worth of chocolate. There's this place, Angelina, where they serve the most delightful hot chocolate. The best thing you've ever tasted in your life. It's like drinking a chocolate bar!"

"Mmmm . . . chocolate," Bess said. She raised her eyebrows at Nancy.

"In fact, I brought you back some as a thank-you." Miss Bouret held up a gold box in her hands. "You took such great care of my beautiful babies. I wasn't sure if I could leave them for two weeks, especially with the annual Garden Society Show just around the corner. But they look better than they ever have.  Thank you, Nancy. Or as they say in French . . . *merci!*" She leaned over and kissed Nancy on both cheeks.

"You're very welcome. I was happy to, really." Nancy blushed. She looked down at the gold box in her hands. It was decorated with a bright pink bow.

"Tell us more about France," George said. She inched closer to Mimsy. They always loved hearing about her travels. When she went to Africa the previous year, they'd listened to her talk about the lion pride she saw on safari. She'd spotted hippos and monkeys, and even come within a few feet of a giraffe.

Miss Bouret stared off and smiled. "Oh, it was just . . . mesmerizing. I found a little cheese shop on the Seine. I must've sat there for hours, talking to the waiters and tasting everything in the place. Paris is just divine. You girls will have to go once you're old enough." She clasped her hands to her heart. It was then Nancy noticed she was holding a thick beige card.

"What's that?" Nancy asked.

"This?" Mimsy said, holding it up. "It's the other part of your thank-you present. You're all invited."

Mimsy handed Nancy the thick piece of paper. Bess and George huddled around her. *You're Invited to the 16th Annual Garden Society Show*, it read. Nancy scanned the details. The event was taking place next weekend at Le Chateau, one of the fanciest spots in River Heights. Nancy had heard of it only once before—it was where her second cousin had gotten married.

"There'll be bouquets from all over the

state," Mimsy said. "If that doesn't convince you, you'll be swayed by the desserts. This year the famous pastry chef Jean-Claude will be there. He's coming all the way from New York City."

"I've seen him on the cooking channel!" George cried. "That guy is famous."

"Indeed he is," Mimsy said. "I'd love for you girls to come as my VIP guests."

Bess bit her lip. "What do you mean, VIP?"

"It means we're very important people." George smiled. She bounced up and down on her toes as she said it.

"Yes, very important," Mimsy agreed. "Because of you, Nancy, I have a chance of winning first place in the Rose Garden. My roses are more impressive than they have been in years. I might actually beat Mrs. Geraldine DeWitt, and she wins *every* year. So what do you say, will you be my guests?"

The girls glanced sideways at each other. A famous chef, beautiful flowers, and the fanciest country club in all of River Heights. It wasn't even a question. "Yes!" the girls cried together.

Nancy held the invitation in the air. She hadn't been this excited since the first day of summer vacation. "Of course we will. Yes!"

ChaPTER TWo

Friendly Competition

The volleyball flew over the net. It was headed right for Nancy's face. At the last second she hit it with both hands. The ball arced up and over the net, just inches from Deirdre Shannon. She'd barely reached out when it bounced off the floor. "And that's the game!" Mrs. Velez, the River Heights Elementary gym teacher, yelled. She blew her whistle. "The score is ten to eight. Nancy, Bess, and George win this one."

Deirdre scrunched her nose like she'd just smelled something rotten. Behind her, her friend Suzie Park crossed her arms over her chest. Nancy and her friends had had enough gym classes with them to know how competitive they were. Most of the time they were okay, but they *hated* losing. They'd thrown tantrums last week when they lost a tennis match. They talked to Mrs. Velez right up until the bell rang, arguing that the other team had cheated.

George pulled Nancy and Bess away, changing the subject before Deirdre could say anything to them. "So I finally picked out my dress for the Garden Society Show," she said. "It's blue and shimmery."

Nancy grabbed her knapsack from the bleachers. Then she pulled her sweaty hair back into a ponytail. "I can't wait to see it. Hannah wants me to wear the dress I wore to the Spring Fling last year."

Bess slung her backpack over one shoulder. The girls had known Hannah, the Drews' housekeeper, for a long time. After Nancy's mom died, Hannah had helped Nancy's dad look after her. She was the one who made them snacks after school or drove them to the movies on the weekends. "I love that dress. This party

11

is going to be incredible. Just us, unlimited desserts, and a room full of flowers. There's no way it won't be fun."

"Are you talking about the Garden Society Show?" a voice asked. The girls turned around to see Deirdre and Suzie standing just a few feet behind them. Deirdre's cheeks were still flushed from the volleyball game.

Nancy glanced sideways at her friends. "That's the one. . . . Why?"

Deirdre laughed. "Is this your first time going? We go every year. My aunt is Geraldine DeWitt. Her roses always win—*always*. I don't know why they even bother having the competition."

Bess grabbed Nancy's arm. "Isn't that the woman Miss Bouret was talking about?" she whispered. Nancy nodded, remembering the name.

Three volleyball games were finishing up behind them. Girls sprinted across the courts, kneeling down to hit shots back over the net. Mrs. Velez blew her whistle twice more. "Great then," Nancy said. She tried hard to sound cheerful. "We'll see you there." The last thing she wanted was to get into a fight with Deirdre. She was one of the meanest girls at River Heights Elementary. Just when Nancy thought she'd been wrong about Deirdre, that maybe they could be friends, Deirdre would do something to change Nancy's mind. Sometimes it was just a rude comment, but other times she'd actually made fun of Bess or George.

Nancy turned to go, but Deirdre followed them. "So how did you three get an invite?" she asked.

George stood up straight. "We're going as Mimsy Bouret's *VIP* guests."

Suzie whispered something to Deirdre and they both laughed. "VIP, huh?"

"That's right," Bess said. She tucked her thumbs under the straps of her backpack.

"I've never heard of a VIP guest at the Garden Society Show. There's just the winners . . . and everyone else. Like your friend."

"Well, maybe Miss Bouret will win this year. Everyone's saying her roses are the most impressive they've ever been. She might be taking first place this year," Bess added.

"I really doubt that," Deirdre said.

Nancy looked at the clock. In one minute the period would be over. They'd be free to go. It was miserable standing here listening to Deirdre brag about her aunt and question them about their invitation. Why did Deirdre care so much anyway? Everyone liked to win. It didn't matter if it was some silly bike race or a volleyball game. But was winning really *everything*?

"We'll see you on Saturday," Nancy said, turning to her friends. She widened her eyes, as if to say, *Come on, let's get out of here.* Bess and George followed her toward the door just as the bell rang.

"I cannot wait," Deirdre called out.

When Nancy looked back, Suzie and Deirdre were smiling and laughing. Nancy swore she heard them say something mean under their breath.

"Don't worry, Miss Bouret is definitely going to win," Bess whispered. "You heard her. Her roses are the best they've been in years."

But Nancy still felt a little uneasy. She and her friends had been looking forward to the Garden Society Show all week. They'd picked out their outfits, painted their nails, and imagined all kinds of crazy desserts. Now that Deirdre and Suzie were coming, it was definitely going to change things.

Nancy only hoped it would be for better, not for worse.

CHAPTER THREE

The Missing Blooms

"Voilà!" Mimsy cried as they stepped into the Grand Ballroom of Le Chateau. It was the fanciest place Nancy and her friends had ever seen. Marble pillars lined the entranceway. A statue of a woman stood above a stone fountain. The ceiling was painted with clouds, and everywhere they turned there were flowers, hundreds of bouquets of every color and size.

A waiter in a tuxedo and white gloves strode up to the girls. "Would you like some caviar?" he asked.

"What's that?" Bess whispered.

Mimsy picked up a thin cracker. It was covered with tiny orange globes. "Fish eggs. A deli-

cacy," she said. Then she popped it in her mouth.

Nancy and George scrunched their noses. "Fish eggs?" George said under her breath. "Gross!"

"You may not like caviar," Miss Bouret said, "but I'm sure you'll like that." She pointed across the Grand Ballroom. There, in the center of a pile of cookies, stood a four-foot-tall chocolate fountain. People huddled around it. They dipped in pieces of cake, strawberries, and slices of banana.

Bess ran over, Nancy and George trailing right behind her. She picked up one of the fruit skewers and dipped it in the chocolate waterfall. "This is the best fountain I've ever seen," she said. When she took a bite, her brown eyes looked like they might pop out of her head. "Much better than the water fountains at school."

Nancy and George dipped pound cake and vanilla cookies into the chocolate. Nancy had never tasted anything so good. Together they made all sorts of combinations. They made chocolate with bananas, chocolate with mint cookies, and chocolate with strawberries.

"The pineapple is the best," Bess said. She popped another piece of fruit in her mouth.

The girls glanced around the Grand Ballroom. It was as big as a football field. Across the way, Mimsy chatted with a woman holding a bouquet of tulips. Mimsy was still fixing her hair. She'd driven the girls to the show this morning in her bright blue convertible. Nancy had begged her dad for permission to ride to the show with Mimsy, and he'd finally agreed, but only if he came at five o'clock to take the girls home.

Next to Mimsy, a few ladies huddled around a vase of purple hydrangeas. Some pinched the petals. The man beside Nancy dunked another cookie into the fountain. "And this is only the beginning!" He laughed. "Be sure to save room for Jean-Claude's famous chocolate mousse cake. Apparently it takes over a week to prepare." When he smiled, Nancy noticed a clump of chocolate in his gray beard.

"I'm starting to get a stomachache," Bess groaned.

"Look at those," George said, distracted. She pointed to a table filled with bright pink orchids. The girls strolled over, getting within a few inches of the flowering plants.

An older woman with thick black glasses stepped beside them. "So, you have discovered my phalaenopsis!" The woman clapped her hands as she said it.

"Phal—who?" Nancy asked. That was one flower Miss Bouret didn't have. Nancy hadn't heard of anything like it.

"They're sometimes called moth orchids," the woman said. She pointed to the bright pink flower in the center. "This particular one grows upside down, under a canopy of trees. That way it's protected from direct sunlight. I'd show you how, but I don't want to flip over the pot. The judging is going to start soon."

The girls leaned forward, their noses just inches from the flower. "It does kind of look like a moth . . . ," George said as she studied the petals.

"But much cooler . . . ," Bess added.

A redhead with glasses strode by. She paused in front of the plants. "Would you like a picture with Mrs. Hamilton's famous orchid?" She held up a camera with a long lens.

Nancy wrapped her arms around her friends. Mrs. Hamilton stood behind them, posed next to her pink orchid. They all smiled as the photographer snapped away. When the photos were done, Nancy and her friends looked at world-famous lilies, then at pictures of the winning bouquets from last year. They tasted some of the best appetizers, like brie cheese and coconut shrimp. They were so busy eating chicken skewers they hardly noticed Deirdre and Suzie as they strolled by arm in arm.

"So happy you're here," Deirdre said. But she didn't sound happy. Suzie hovered right behind her, like they were connected. "That's my aunt Geraldine . . . and her famous roses." She pointed at a table across the way. A woman with a tight gray bun and red lipstick hovered over two bouquets. Each was filled with pink roses, the petals a little purple around the edges. Nancy, Bess, and George had never seen award-winning roses before. They looked too perfect to be real.

"They are pretty," Bess admitted.

"Miss Bouret was just here a minute ago," Nancy said as she looked around. It took them a moment to spot Mimsy, even with her bright dress and floral scarf. She was surrounded by people. She held up her bouquet of peach roses as a few of her friends looked on.

"These are extraordinary!" a blond woman cried. "Your rosebush hasn't flowered like that in years. You'll have to tell me your secret."

A woman with jeweled glasses inched closer. "You're going to take first place this year. It's a crime if you don't." Nancy stared at Mimsy's bouquet, which was nearly twice the size of Geraldine DeWitt's. Each rose was the size of a large apple. She was beginning to think the woman had a point. Maybe Miss Bouret *would* win.

Deirdre crossed her arms over her chest. "My aunt wins every year. Every. Single. Year." She narrowed her eyes at the girls, daring them to say something.

Nancy glanced sideways at her friends. Bess's face was pale. One thing was clear: Deirdre was taking this whole competition way too seriously. Thankfully Helene Flossenhammer, the head of the Garden Society, stepped on the stage at that very moment. Everyone made their way across the Grand Ballroom to hear her speech.

Mimsy stood up front while Nancy, Bess, and George filed in beside her. They lost Deirdre and Suzie somewhere in the crowd. "Welcome to the sixteenth annual Garden Society Show," Helene Flossenhammer said into the microphone. She was one of the tallest women Nancy had ever seen. She wore a large floppy hat that was covered with fake flowers.

"We're all so pleased you could join us. Thank you to Le Chateau for hosting us. We're very lucky to have Jean-Claude, the famous pastry chef, here all the way from New York City." The crowd broke into applause. Nancy turned to the front of the Grand Ballroom, where a man with white hair was standing beside the stage. He barely noticed Helene.

Instead he was whispering to a skinny boy with black hair. Jean-Claude's face was tense, as if each word took great effort to get out. Nancy could barely hear what he was saying. "You never do anything right," he huffed. "How many times do I have to tell you? Egg whites! No yolks! Baking is a science, a real science! Anything less than perfection is not good enough." The boy was blushing so much his ears turned red.

Helene kept talking. She went through the list of judges, who had come to the show for the last ten years. She thanked friends of the Garden Society who had donated gift baskets and certificates for their raffle. At one point she pulled Geraldine DeWitt onstage. She congratulated her on winning Bloom of the Year five times in a row. When Helene was nearly done she turned to the three judges. They all held clipboards in their hands, their pens resting on paper. "And now we'll start the judging. Winners will be announced tonight at the Garden Society Gala. Good luck to all!"

"Gala? Does that mean party?" George asked.

"You bet it does." Mimsy laughed. "There's going to be a formal dinner tonight at eight for just adults. That's when the real celebrating will happen. Now if you'll excuse me, ladies . . . I need to go stand beside my blooms!" Mimsy smiled as she disappeared into the crowd. Nancy had never seen her so happy. It was like she'd already won the first-place ribbon.

"Where'd Deirdre and Suzie go?" Bess asked, looking around.

Nancy scanned the Grand Ballroom. She didn't see the girls anywhere. "I'm not sure. Maybe they've discovered the chocolate fountain." Nancy giggled as she walked toward the dessert table. They'd spend the afternoon eating sweets and taking pictures with all the amazing flowers. Some of them she'd never seen before. They looked like they'd been flown in from the Amazon rain forest.

Nancy and Bess were reaching for chocolate strawberries when someone screamed. The girls turned around. There, across the room, was Mimsy Bouret. Her face was completely white. She covered her heart with her hand.

"What is it? What happened?" Helene called out from the stage.

Mimsy pointed to an empty vase. "Someone stole my roses!" she yelled. "They're gone!"

chaPTER FOUR

Ticktock, Ticktock

"Now, now," Helene Flossenhammer said. She paced back and forth in front of the empty vase. "Calm down, Mimsy. There has to be an explanation for this."

A small crowd had formed around the table. Nancy, Bess, and George stood in front, watching the scene unfold. Mimsy's cheeks were deep red and she looked a little out of breath.

"I just stepped away for a few minutes," she

said. "I went up to the stage to listen to your welcome speech. I was there the whole time. When I came back they were gone. The whole bouquet has disappeared!"

One of the judges wore a dark gray suit. "Could someone have taken them somewhere? Maybe someone wanted to give them a last-minute pruning before the judging started. Did you have anyone with you?"

Mimsy looked to Nancy and her friends. "You girls didn't move them, did you?" she asked hopefully.

"I'm sorry, Miss Bouret," Nancy said sadly. "But we were watching Helene's speech too. We haven't touched them at all. The last time I saw them was when you had them before Helene spoke, but that was nearly half an hour ago."

Helene Flossenhammer looked down the row of judges. Then she glanced at her watch. "I feel bad, I do, Mimsy. But if we don't start the judging soon, we might not finish in time for the gala tonight."

"Someone must've stolen them." Mimsy rubbed her hand over her forehead. "I don't know what else could have happened."

Two of the judges furrowed their brows, as if they didn't quite believe Mimsy's story. A woman with a bright green scarf shook her head. "Whatever the case is, we need to begin. If you find the bouquet by the gala tonight, we'll include it in the competition. We'll be announcing the winners at eight o'clock."

With that, the judges stepped away. They walked over to the Orchid Garden and scribbled something on their clipboards. Helene was the last to go. "I wish this hadn't happened, Mimsy. Good luck," she whispered. Then she followed behind the judges.

The rest of the crowd left. Some circled tables of lilies, while others piled their plates with cookies and fruit. When they were finally alone Mimsy looked down at the girls. "I'm telling the truth," she said. "I don't know what else to say. They were right here . . . and then they weren't.

Who would do something like this?" She pulled a tissue from her pocket. She pressed it to her eyes, dabbing away tears.

"I don't know, but we're going to find out," Nancy said. "I promise."

Nancy grabbed Miss Bouret's hand, trying to make her feel better. Mimsy looked forward to the Garden Society Show all year. She spent hours in her yard, planting and watering her flowers. For months leading up to it, it seemed like all she talked about was the special fertilizer she used or how humming to her plants helped them grow. Gardening was one of her favorite things to do. Nancy hated to see her so upset. Worst of all, she knew Mimsy would never lie. Not about this.

George looked at her watch. "It's eleven o'clock now. That means we have nine hours before the gala tonight. As long as we can find the bouquet before the winners are announced, Miss Bouret will still have a chance to win."

"Oh dear," Mimsy said. "I don't even know

where to begin. How am I going to find out who did this? I might as well forget it. . . ."

"Don't give up just yet," Bess said. She pulled a small notebook out of her back pocket. "It's time for the Clue Crew to do what we do best."

Nancy looked at her friends and smiled. "It's time to solve this mystery," she said.

ChaPTER FiVE

Unusual Suspects

Nancy paced back and forth in front of the table. "Let's look for clues," she said quietly. As she examined the scene, she noticed there were drops of water on one side of the empty vase. "Someone must have pulled them out of the vase and gone that way," Nancy said. She pointed toward the back of the Grand Ballroom. "That's where the drops of water lead."

Bess leaned down to look at the table. Nancy was right. There were six drops of water in a straight line. They must have come off the roses when they were taken out of the vase. "Maybe someone ran for the back exit?"

Bess wrote in her notebook. "If it's eleven o'clock now, when were the roses taken?" she asked.

The girls looked to Mimsy for an answer. "Well, I was one of the last people to go to the stage," Mimsy said. "The speech started right around ten thirty. I remember because I looked at my watch."

"The roses were taken between ten thirty and a little before eleven," George said. Bess scribbled another note in her book.

"And you're sure they disappeared from this table? This vase?" Nancy asked.

"One hundred percent," Mimsy said. She held her face in her hands.

Nancy studied the vase. It was one of the nicest ones on the table. It was clear glass with a pattern cut into it. Nancy had only ever seen ones like it at her grandmother's house, and she was never allowed to touch those. "Is the vase very expensive?" she asked.

Mimsy nodded. "Very. It doesn't make any

sense that someone would take the roses and not the vase. That's worth ten times as much as a bunch of flowers."

George put her hands on her hips. "Motive," she said. "Isn't that the word for why someone does something? Whoever did this must have been afraid your roses would win the show."

Bess wrote *motive* across the top of a page. "You're right. I can't think of any other reason someone would take them. Especially when they left the vase here."

"There are three people here who have a motive, then." George pointed across the Grand Ballroom. Deirdre and Suzie stood next to Deirdre's aunt Geraldine. They were all smiling as they ate dainty sandwiches from a silver tray. "Is there anyone else you can think of?"

"Hmmmm . . . I don't know," Mimsy said. "I hate to accuse anyone, but Geraldine is my only real competition. At least that's what everyone has been saying. But still . . . would they have really done something like this?"

"Maybe," Bess said. She wrote three suspects down in her notebook. *Geraldine DeWitt, Deirdre,* and *Suzie.* "You never know."

"It just seems hopeless," Mimsy said. She leaned against the table as if she felt dizzy. "Even if she did take them, she would never admit to it."

"Don't worry, Miss Bouret," Nancy said. "We'll figure this out."

The girls strode across the Grand Ballroom toward Deirdre. The photographer snapped more pictures of the guests. A woman in a puffy blue dress posed with her orchids. Two older women held their shrimp in the air.

"The cucumber and cream cheese sandwiches are the best," Deirdre said. She bit into another one. Suzie Park nibbled on a ham and cheese one. They both turned around when they noticed Nancy and her friends.

"Too bad about Mimsy's roses," Suzie said, and laughed.

"Guess there's always next year, right?"

Deirdre smiled wickedly. She was definitely happy the roses had vanished . . . but was she the one who took them?

"Yes, such a tragedy," Geraldine went on. Nancy couldn't tell if she really cared or not. As she spoke she rearranged her bouquet, moving some of the bigger roses to the front. "Who would do such a thing?"

Bess held her notebook in the air. "That's what we're trying to figure out."

Nancy leaned in to question them. "Did you see anything strange this morning? Where were you when Helene gave her speech?"

Geraldine tapped her fingers on the table. "No, I can't say I did. When Helene took the stage, I was standing to the right of it, beside Mrs. Canter. We talked a little about her lilacs. Then I listened to Helene's speech. Deirdre and Suzie were there with me the whole time."

"Did you see anything strange?" Nancy asked Deirdre. She was feeling more suspicious of Deirdre than usual. Everyone knew Deirdre hated losing. But would she really steal Mimsy's roses? That seemed a little extreme, even for her.

"Nothing I can think of," Deirdre said. She took another bite of her sandwich.

"Do you remember when you first heard the roses were missing?" Bess asked.

"Probably when Mimsy screamed. I bet people two towns over heard that." Deirdre laughed.

Just then a woman with a short white bob strolled up, a vase of purple lilacs in one hand. "These are them, Geraldine," she said. "The judges seemed impressed."

"As they should be!" Geraldine said. She put her nose just a few inches from the flowers and breathed in. "They smell wonderful, and they look even better."

Nancy remembered what Geraldine had said about Mrs. Canter, the woman she was standing with. "Were you with Mrs. DeWitt and the girls during Helene's speech?"

"Yes . . . ," the woman said. She looked confused.

"And they were right beside you the whole time?" Nancy pressed.

Mrs. Canter laughed. "Yes. Why?"

Nancy didn't want to offend anyone, but investigating sometimes meant ruling out suspects. "We just wanted to be sure," she said

Geraldine put her hands on her hips. "You

don't think any of us would steal Mimsy's roses, do you? What kind of people do you think we are?"

Bess tried to explain. "No, but you're Miss Bouret's competition. We're trying to figure out why someone would take the flowers. It doesn't make any sense."

At this, Geraldine seemed angry. She pressed her bright red lips into a thin line. "Well, I've never been so offended! Me? A criminal? Why aren't you questioning Tessa Fitzgerald?"

Nancy shared a look with her friends. They'd never even heard that name before. Not from Mimsy or anyone else. "Who?" George asked.

Geraldine pointed across the Grand Ballroom. An older couple stood near the back exit. The woman was wearing a pink ball gown and matching shawl. They looked like they were arguing. "Tessa Fitzgerald!" Geraldine cried. "She's the one saying she saw someone take the flowers. Why aren't you asking her these questions?"

Deirdre and Suzie looked annoyed. "Yeah," Deirdre huffed. "If you're such amazing detectives, why are you blaming us?"

"We're just trying to get to the bottom of this," Nancy tried. "We're not blaming anyone."

George pulled Nancy away before Deirdre could go on. They took off across the Grand Ballroom, dodging a few waiters with silver trays. "That didn't go well," Bess whispered.

"I think it went great," Nancy said. She didn't take her eyes off the couple by the exit. "It's official. We have our first witness. . . ."

ChAPTER Six

He Said, She Said

Nancy and her friends walked to the back of the Grand Ballroom. Bess pointed to the table where the roses were taken. It wasn't even ten feet away from where the couple stood. "See?" Bess said. "If they were here when it happened, they had the perfect view."

George put her finger over her lips, telling the girls to be quiet. She nodded in the direction of the woman. She was arguing with her husband about something. George, Bess, and Nancy inched closer until they could hear.

"But he wasn't young," the man said. He shoved his hands into the pockets of his suit pants. "He was losing his hair."

The woman shook her thick gray curls. "Gregory, I know what I saw. The man definitely wasn't bald. I know that for a fact."

Nancy cleared her throat—something her father did whenever he wanted to get someone's attention. The couple stopped arguing and turned to look at the girls. "Excuse me," Nancy said. "Are you Tessa Fitzgerald? We heard you saw who took the missing roses."

The man rolled his eyes. "She's Tessa

and I'm her husband, Gregory Fitzgerald. For the record, we both saw who took them."

"We need your help, then. What did he look like?" Bess asked.

Mrs. Fitzgerald let out a sigh. "He was wearing a blue shirt. He had a mustache maybe, or a goatee . . ."

"He didn't have a goatee," Mr. Fitzgerald said. "Not at all. He was wearing a black jacket."

George took a turn with the notebook. Bess had flipped to a clean page, but she hadn't written anything on it. Their only two witnesses couldn't agree on what they saw. "Let's start from the beginning," George tried. "Can you tell us what happened? When did you notice the man who took the flowers?"

Mr. Fitzgerald nodded. "Well, we stood in the back during the speech. I just hate crowds. I need my own space, you know?"

"Yes, and while we were back here we noticed this man taking away a bouquet of roses. I thought they were his," Mrs. Fitzgerald added.

Mr. Fitzgerald held one finger in the air. "He was older and practically bald. I think he might've had gray hair, even."

Mrs. Fitzgerald tapped George's notebook. "Don't write that down. My husband has very bad eyesight, but he refuses to get glasses. The man was young. I know he was."

As Mr. and Mrs. Fitzgerald argued, Nancy, Bess, and George huddled together. "What are we going to do?" Bess whispered. "They can't agree on anything."

Nancy knew this sometimes happened. Witnesses could have very different descriptions of what they saw. Mrs. Fitzgerald thought the man was wearing just a blue shirt, but her husband thought he was wearing a jacket. Mrs. Fitzgerald swore he had facial hair but her husband thought that was wrong. Nancy hoped they could agree on at least one fact.

"Do you remember what time this happened?" she asked.

"Well, it happened just ten minutes before

the speech ended," Mr. Fitzgerald said.

"Maybe fifteen minutes," Mrs. Fitzgerald argued. George looked at the notebook and let out a sigh. She still hadn't written anything down. Their witnesses weren't helping much.

"I'm sure about one thing. It happened right after we took that photo," Mr. Fitzgerald said.

"What photo?" Nancy asked.

"The photographer came by and took a photo of us," Mrs. Fitzgerald agreed. "Then we saw the man. It happened no more than a minute later."

"The photographer!" Nancy cried. "This is perfect."

"What about the photographer?" Bess asked. She looked confused.

George tapped her pen against the top of the notebook. She knew exactly what Nancy meant. "If the photographer was here just before the roses were taken, she may have gotten a picture of the man who took them. We need to see her photos."

Mrs. Fitzgerald leaned down so she was eye level with the girls. "I'm truly sorry we couldn't be of more help."

"You've been a huge help, really," Nancy replied. She meant every word. Even if Mr. and Mrs. Fitzgerald couldn't agree, they'd given the Clue Crew their first big lead. If they could find the photographer, they might be able to solve the case with time to spare.

Nancy scanned the Grand Ballroom. Jean-Claude and his assistant wheeled out another cart stacked with jelly cookies, tiny cupcakes, and fruit tarts. The judges strolled through the Lily Garden. Mimsy sat in the corner with another woman. She still looked like she might burst into tears at any moment.

"I don't see the photographer," Nancy said.

Bess shook her head. "Me neither. She was here all morning, why would she suddenly leave?"

The girls left Mr. and Mrs. Fitzgerald near the back exits. They weaved through waiters and guests. They looked by the Tulip Garden and the Lily Garden, but they didn't see the photographer anywhere. They could still hear Mr. and Mrs. Fitzgerald arguing as they moved deeper into the crowd.

ChaPTER SEVEN

Caught in the Act

After an hour Nancy, Bess, and George stood behind a boy, staring at the card in his hands. "Is that what I think it is?" Bess asked. "Look at the tiny camera symbol on the business card. That has to be from the photographer, right?"

Nancy nodded. The girls had spent the last hour circling the Grand Ballroom, trying to find the redheaded woman with the camera, but she'd disappeared. She was no longer taking pictures of the Orchid Garden or asking people to pose by the Rose Garden bouquets. Now the only trace of her was a few business cards she'd given out. They'd spotted the boy, who was blond with freckles, sitting alone at a table. Nancy figured he was someone's nephew or grandson. He looked like he was about to pass out from boredom.

"Excuse us," Nancy said as she went over to the table. It was covered with a lace cloth and plates of half-eaten cake. "Did you get that card from the photographer?"

The boy spun around. He couldn't have been older than twelve, but he looked a little nervous when he saw them. "Whoa. Aren't you the girls looking for the stolen roses? Just for the record, I didn't take them."

"We didn't think you did," Bess said. She

nearly laughed. Apparently word of their investigation had gotten around. "We're more curious about that card you have."

"What about it?" the boy asked. He wore a nice shirt and a bow tie. The tie was fastened crooked. "What does the photographer have to do with anything?"

Bess pointed to Mr. and Mrs. Fitzgerald. They strolled around the hydrangeas, stopping to smell some of the bouquets. "We have two witnesses who saw a man take the flowers. But they can't agree on what he looked like. We're hoping the photographer has a picture of him."

"I haven't seen her for at least an hour, maybe more than that," the boy said. "She took a picture of me and my grandma Helene. Then she gave us this card. She wants to take pictures at my grandma's seventieth birthday party."

"You're Helene Flossenhammer's grandson?" George asked.

"Yup," the boy said. "My mom makes me come to the show every year with her and my dad. Boooooorrrrrrrring." He pretended to fall asleep.

George glanced down at the notebook. When she'd gotten tired looking for the photographer she took a break. She'd drawn two pictures of the "suspect." In one she used the description Mrs. Fitzgerald had given them. In the other she'd used the description Mr. Fitzgerald had given. "Do either of these people look familiar to you?" she asked, knowing it was a long shot.

The boy shook his head. "Not at all," he mumbled.

Bess let out a sigh. They had looked everywhere for the photographer. They'd walked through every flower garden. They'd seen gardenias, lilacs, orchids, roses, and more. They'd asked every waiter in the Grand Ballroom if they'd seen the woman with the camera. It was almost like she'd vanished into thin air.

Nancy plucked the card from the boy's hand. "Jenna Crosby," she read. At least they had her phone number now, in case they needed it.

"She must've left the Garden Show," George said. "Should we search the rest of Le Chateau?"

Nancy raised her eyebrows. "Do you think she could be hiding out somewhere in the rest of the building? How many parties are happening this afternoon?"

"I bet there's a ton," the boy chimed in. "But I could help you find her. You'll have a better chance if you have one more person looking with you." He looked around the room at the older crowd. Most of the people were women. Nearly everyone had gray hair. "Please? I might die of boredom if I don't."

Nancy looked to her friends. She'd never considered a full search of Le Chateau, and she'd definitely never considered letting Helene Flossenhammer's grandson help them. But the building was huge, with parties of all sorts going on inside it. She knew they weren't supposed to leave the Garden Society Show, but how would they find their next clue if they didn't? Wasn't it worth the risk?

"Let's try it," Nancy said.

The boy sprang from his seat like a jack-in-the-box. "Great! I promise you won't regret this! I'll really help you guys out, I swear. I'm Adam, by the way. Adam Flossenhammer."

Bess and George exchanged a nervous look. There was a reason the Clue Crew was only three people—it was easier that way. "Okay, Adam . . . ," Bess said. "You search the west wing and we'll search the east wing."

"Suh-weeet!" Adam yelped.

Then the girls took off toward the opposite exit. They waved to Adam as they slipped out the side doors.

"Do you see anything?" Bess whispered.

Nancy pulled back the curtain a tiny bit more. They were hiding in one of the Le Chateau's side rooms. The hallway had ended with a velvet curtain. Now they were behind it, trying to look inside.

Nancy stared into the ballroom. It was filled

with people dressed in fancy gowns and tuxedos. Ten girls in neon green dresses wandered about. A woman with short black hair stepped onto the dance floor. She wore a puffy white dress and held her husband's hand. "Introducing Mr. and Mrs. Kim!" the announcer yelled. The couple came together for a slow dance.

"Just a wedding," Nancy said. They crept back down the hall, looking for another party.

Le Chateau was a maze of hallways and ballrooms. They'd been searching for over an hour. They'd already found a cocktail party and a private dinner with men in suits. They were walking through an empty dining room when they heard Adam's voice.

"Psssst! I found her! She's photographing another party!" Adam appeared at the end of the hall. "Over here!" He waved his arms frantically, like he was signaling a plane.

The girls chased after him. They followed Adam down two long hallways. The music grew louder as they came closer to sliding glass doors. Adam stood beside the window.

There was a party on the lawn outside. A jazz band played a happy song. The saxophonist knelt down as he started a solo. A few people danced in a half circle, clapping their hands to the beat. "See?" Adam asked. "Isn't that her?" He pointed to a woman just ten feet from the door. She had bright red hair and black glasses. She held a camera with a long lens.

"You're right!" Nancy said.

"We have to talk to her," George tried. She slid the door open a few inches, trying not to draw too much attention to them. "Excuse us! Jenna Crosby! Were you working the Garden Society Show?"

Jenna froze. She turned, not sure where the voice had come from. She looked confused when she spotted the four kids huddled around the doors. "Why do you ask? I finished up there hours ago." She let her camera fall to her side.

Nancy took a deep breath. "We were hoping to see your pictures. We think you may have caught someone stealing one of the prized bouquets."

Jenna stepped inside, glancing over her shoulder to make sure no one was watching her. "I'm supposed to be working right now," she whispered. "Can't you find me later?"

"We don't have much time," George tried. "Our friend can't enter the show until we find out who stole her roses. We think you can help."

Jenna looked back to the party, like she wasn't sure what to do. Then she stepped inside and shut the door behind her. "Okay, but we'll have to hurry. Do you know when they were taken?"

"Between ten thirty and eleven." George read from the notes. "And there should be a picture of a gray-haired woman in a pink ball gown before or after it."

Jenna turned the camera so the kids could see the screen. She hit an arrow beside the small window, scrolling through each photo. There were tons of pictures of people dancing. There were even more of the jazz band.

After a few minutes they reached the photos of the Garden Society Show. Geraldine posed for a picture with Helene. The photographer had taken photos of guests and nearly every bouquet. They even saw the picture of Adam with his parents and his grandmother. He was making a silly face.

"There they are!" Nancy cried. They'd finally reached the photo of Mr. and Mrs. Fitzgerald.

They were standing right in front of Mimsy's roses. The bouquet was in the vase, just as Mimsy had described.

"Can you go back?" Bess asked.

Jenna went to the picture before. Sure enough, the roses were gone. At the edge of the picture they saw a man in a white jacket. He held the roses close to his side. "I can only see the side of his face, but I can zoom in on the jacket," Jenna said. She hit a few buttons and a gold symbol came into view. It looked like initials, but it was too far away to be sure.

"Have you seen that jacket before? Do you know who it is?" Nancy asked.

Jenna shook her head. "I don't." She turned back to the party. A man was waving her outside. He looked annoyed. "I have to go now. I'm sorry. Good luck!" She opened the door and warm air rushed in. Nancy could tell it was getting late. The sun was setting in the sky.

"See!" Adam yelped. "I told you I'd be able to find her. Awesome."

But Nancy was too busy thinking of that jacket to notice. "Who would wear that?" Nancy asked. "I don't remember seeing anyone in it."

"Me neither," Bess said.

They strode down the long hallway, back toward the Garden Society Show. Adam trailed behind them, occasionally saying how "cool" it was that he'd been able to help, and how this was the most fun he'd ever had at a Garden Show. The Clue Crew looked at every waiter and guest they passed, but none of them was the man from the photo.

"Whoever that is, we need to find him," Nancy said when they finally reached the Grand Ballroom. It was getting late, and there were even more people in the crowd than before. The clock in the front of the room read four fifteen. They had less than an hour until the show ended and everyone went home. Then there would be no witnesses, no suspects, and no clues to collect before the big gala.

"I know . . ." George trailed off. "But how?"

ChaPTeR EighT

The Mystery Man

"At least you tried," Mimsy said. "Thank you, girls. I don't know what I would've done without you." She dabbed at her eyes with her lace handkerchief. A few feet away, the judges were moving through the Rose Garden. They stopped at Geraldine DeWitt's vases. A man scribbled on his clipboard as he leaned closer.

Nancy glanced toward the exit. Her father, Carson Drew, was there, standing by the front doors of Le Chateau, looking at pictures from the previous year's Garden Society Show. Her father worked as a lawyer and was still wearing his navy suit, even though it was five o'clock on a Saturday. He'd worked overtime before picking the girls up. "We're not going to give up yet," Nancy said. "You never know. Maybe we'll figure this out before the gala. We still have a few hours left."

Bess rested her hands on her cheeks. "But we've searched everywhere," she said. "I haven't seen anyone with that jacket. No one remembered seeing a man who fit that description."

Nancy shrugged. She knew her friends were right. They had searched the Grand Ballroom for the last half hour and found nothing. They'd talked to as many people as they could, asking if they'd seen the man from the picture. They'd even described the white jacket with the gold symbol on the back. Nancy knew it was time to go home, but she wasn't ready to give up.

"Maybe there's a clue we missed," she said.

She looked at the vase and the bouquets on either side of it. There was nothing unusual underneath the table or behind it.

Just then Mr. Drew strode over to them. He'd been waiting by the exit for nearly fifteen minutes. "Dad, can we please have a little more time?" Nancy asked. She held up one finger, as if to say *just one more minute?* "We're so close to figuring this out. Right, Miss Bouret?"

Mimsy wiped her nose with her handkerchief. "You've done terrific work, but I have to get back to my house and get ready for the gala. I guess I'll have to wait for another show. Maybe with your help, the blooms will be just as impressive next year."

Mr. Drew rested his hand on Mimsy's arm, trying to make her feel better. "I'm terribly sorry, Mimsy," he said. "I wish we could've helped more. What kind of person would do this?"

Nancy glanced sideways at Bess and George. They knew exactly what kind of person would do this: a white-jacket-wearing, brown-haired man with shiny black shoes. The only trouble was *finding* him.

Mimsy leaned down to hug Nancy. "Thank you for being my guests. You put the 'important' in 'very important people.' I don't know what I would've done without you." She gave a hug to Bess, then George.

"Thanks for inviting us," Bess said sadly, before heading to the door.

As the three girls walked out, they turned one last time to look at Mimsy. She said good-bye to a few of her friends, then collected her empty vase. She kept staring at it as she headed out a side door toward the parking lot.

"I just don't understand," Bess said. "Our suspect has to be somewhere. How could someone just vanish like that?"

She grabbed a cookie from the plate. Even after hours of eating piles and piles of desserts, Bess was still in the mood for Hannah's home-made chocolate chip cookies. Hannah knew how to make them just right, so they were crispy on the outside and gooey on the inside.

George reviewed the notes. "Was it possible the jacket was a disguise?" she asked Bess and Nancy, who sat across from her at Nancy's kitchen table. Mr. Drew had dropped them off at the house, then returned to work. It was already six thirty. There were less than two hours left until the gala started, and they were no closer to solving the mystery.

"It might've been. Maybe we could find out where he got the disguise from," Nancy said. "Even that would be helpful."

Behind them, Hannah moved around the Drews' kitchen, cleaning the last of the bowls and pans. She grabbed three spoons covered in cookie dough and handed them to the girls. "It sounds like a lot happened today at the Garden Society Show."

"Tons. Someone took Mimsy's rose bouquet," Nancy said.

George flipped through more notes. She

thought about Mr. and Mrs. Fitzgerald's descriptions of the suspect. After all that, it seemed like neither one of them had been right. No one had said anything about a white jacket with a gold symbol on the back. "Is it possible he came from another part of Le Chateau? Maybe the person in the jacket wasn't from our party at all."

"But then why would he want the flowers?" Nancy asked. "Whoever it was knew Mimsy had the chance to win. It just doesn't make any sense."

Bess licked the cookie dough off her spoon, distracted from the conversation. "This is so good, Hannah," she said. "Your cookies are even better than Jean-Claude's."

"Jean-Claude?" Hannah asked. She furrowed her brow.

"He made all the desserts for the party. You probably know him from TV," Bess explained. But Hannah still looked confused, like she'd never heard his name before.

"I'll show you his website," Bess said, getting up from the table. "You'll see!"

As Bess went searching for Nancy's laptop, Nancy and George huddled together. They flipped through the notes, looking for anything that might spark an idea. George studied the page labeled *Motive* for a second time. "Maybe we have the wrong motive. Maybe whoever took the roses didn't know much about Mimsy."

"We haven't ruled out Deirdre and Suzie," Nancy said. "They still could've had something to do with this. Maybe whoever this man is . . . maybe he was just helping—"

"Nancy! George!" Bess's voice called out from the living room. "Come here! Quick!"

Nancy and George jumped from their seats. They knew Bess's excitement could only mean one thing . . . she'd found another clue. "What is it?" George asked.

Bess was on Nancy's laptop. Hannah sat next to her on the Drews' couch, looking at the website Bess had pulled up. It said *Jean-Claude* in fancy script at the top. "Does this look familiar to you?" Bess asked, pointing to the side of the screen.

"I can't believe it!" Nancy cried. On the side of the website was a gold circle with three letters inside. "JCP: Jean-Claude Pastries! It's the same symbol that was on the back of the man's jacket."

"A clue?" Hannah asked. She looked around at the girls' excited faces.

"A definite clue," George agreed. "The man

in the picture must have gotten the jacket from Jean-Claude . . . or he works for him."

Nancy glanced at the clock. "Hannah, we need to go back to Le Chateau," she said. "We have a chance of helping Mimsy find her bouquet. Maybe even before the party starts . . ."

The girls gave Hannah hopeful looks. "Oh, all right," Hannah finally said. She never could resist helping the girls solve a mystery. "Let's go. But if you don't find anything by the party, we head back here . . . and you girls head to bed." She grabbed her coat from the armchair and started toward the door.

"Deal," Nancy said as she pulled her sweater on over her dress. As the three girls followed Hannah to the car, Nancy could think only of Jean-Claude and his assistant. As crazy as it seemed, she was starting to think one of them was to blame. . . .

CHAPTER NINE

A Confession

When the Clue Crew arrived back at Le Chateau, the Grand Ballroom had been completely transformed. It looked like an enchanted forest, with tall trees lining the walls. Blooming bouquets decorated the circular dinner tables. A wooden dance floor had been put down over the carpet. Onstage, a six-piece band set up their instruments. The drummer played a few beats while the first of the guests filed in the front doors.

"Where are they?" Nancy asked, glancing around the room. Jean-Claude's famous mousse cake was on a table in the corner, surrounded by piles of cookies and éclairs. But there were no signs of the chef.

"They must be in the kitchen . . . wherever that is," Bess said. She glanced at the exits.

"Unless they left," George said. She looked scared at the thought.

"I hope not." Nancy pointed toward a side door. "I remember passing the kitchen before, when we were looking for the photographer. I think it's over there. . . ."

As the girls darted across the ballroom, they noticed Helene Flossenhammer fixing place cards on a table. She was half-hidden behind a giant vase of lilies. A few of the judges sat at another table, tallying up the scores. "We have to hurry," Bess whispered. "The rest of the guests will be here soon, and then the judging will be officially over."

Nancy walked faster. She led the girls down a winding hallway and to a giant wooden door. At first they opened it just a crack. Jean-Claude stood at the sink with his assistant, a skinny boy with brown hair. Silver trays and plates were piled up beside them. There were cookie crumbs, dirty dishes, and pans everywhere. The boy washed a bowl. "How many times do I have to tell you, Pierre?" Jean-Claude said in a heavy accent. He held a foil wrapper in his hands. "Dark chocolate, not milk chocolate! Dark chocolate, not milk chocolate! How can I make my masterpieces if I don't have the right supplies? That cake was only average!"

Pierre stared at the bowl. He scrubbed it with a sponge, looking a little embarrassed. "I'm sorry, Jean-Claude," he said quietly.

"Sorry is not good enough. Perfection! That is what I need! Always perfection!" He crumpled the foil into a tight ball and threw it in the trash.

Nancy, Bess, and George stood in the doorway. Nancy didn't like seeing Pierre get yelled at, but she sure liked the jacket he was wearing. The two men couldn't have looked more different. Jean-Claude had spiky gray hair. His face and hands were tan, as if he'd spent all summer in the sun. Pierre was much younger than Jean-Claude. He was tall and thin, with pale skin and dark brown hair. His shoulders were slumped forward.

"It's him," Nancy said. She pointed to Pierre. "The man in the picture had dark brown hair. It was almost black."

Bess and George nodded. Before they could say anything else, Jean-Claude spotted them. "What are you children doing in *my* kitchen? We are one crème brûlée from being done today."

George looked at the floor. "We're trying to find . . . roses."

Pierre bit his fingernail. He seemed nervous now that they had mentioned the missing flowers. "What would I know about roses?" Jean-Claude yelled. He waved his hands, signaling for them to leave. "Please! Enough wasting my time. Out of here."

Nancy cleared her throat. "We think your assistant may have taken roses that belong to our friend. They were prizewinning roses, some of the most valuable ones at the Garden Show today."

Jean-Claude turned to Pierre. Nancy couldn't help but feel sorry for him. Even if he did take the roses, Jean-Claude treated him worse than a misbehaving dog. The girls had been there only a few minutes, and Jean-Claude had been yelling the whole time. "We just want them back," Nancy said.

Pierre shook his head. "I don't know what these kids are talking about." But it was obvious he was lying. He wouldn't look Nancy or her friends in the eye. His hands shook as he washed the bowl. Nancy knew he was the man from the photo . . . but how could she get him to admit it?

"We have a picture of you taking them," Bess said, braver than before.

Jean-Claude narrowed his eyes at the girls. "How dare you come into my kitchen and accuse Jean-Claude! How dare you tell us we have stolen your roses!"

"If you don't know anything about the roses," George said, "then what is that?" She pointed to a far corner of the room. A few peach rose petals and leaves were on the counter.

Bess ran to the counter. "These are definitely them. They're Miss Bouret's all right!"

Nancy clasped her hands together. "Please, we just need to know where they are."

Pierre let out a deep breath. Everyone watched him closely. He dropped the wet bowl in the sink and wiped his hands on his jacket. "Okay, okay, all right. I took them." When he looked at Nancy, he seemed like he was about to cry. "But I can explain. I swear."

Bess held the peach petals in her hands. "You're going to have to."

Pierre sat down on a stool. He put his head in his hands. "I'm so sorry," he said. "I really am. This morning I was supposed to stop at the florist to buy roses to decorate the desserts. We sometimes put flowers on the cakes or cupcakes. The only thing is . . . I forgot."

"You are always forgetting!" Jean-Claude yelled. He pounded the counter with his fist. "I cannot believe this. I told you—"

"I know you told me three times," Pierre went on. "But there was so much to do for the Garden Society Show that I forgot about the roses. And by the time I got here it was too late. I'd already made a mistake with a few of the ingredients. I didn't want to make another. So while everyone was listening to the speeches, I snuck into the ballroom. I didn't think it would matter if I took just one bunch of roses. But I was wrong."

Nancy shook her head. "Miss Bouret was panicked. Why didn't you just tell her you'd taken them?"

Pierre shrugged. "It wasn't until after I used them that I realized they were hers. And then it felt like it was too late. I know it was a mistake. I'm so sorry."

Jean-Claude threw his arms up in the air. "It is too late for sorrys! This is such an embarrassment, Pierre." He huffed about, tossing trays and dishes into the sink.

Nancy looked at the clock on the wall. The gala would begin shortly. Maybe Jean-Claude was wrong. Maybe it wasn't too late to fix things. "Where are the flowers now?" she asked. "Is there a way for Mimsy to show them to the judges?"

Pierre's face lit up. He looked better than he had since they'd shown up. "I hope so," he said. "I can bring you to them now."

"We only have a few minutes until the gala begins," Bess said. She pointed to the clock.

Pierre pulled off his jacket and threw it on the counter. Then he headed for the door. "Come on, then," he called. He waved for them to follow. "We'll have to hurry."

ChaPTER TEN

The Perfect Rose

When they returned to the Grand Ballroom, the clock struck eight o'clock. Guests were pouring into the front entrance, oohing and aahing over the beautiful decorations. Geraldine DeWitt wore a full-length evening gown and ten strands of pearls. Mimsy shuffled in behind her. She was dressed in a silk dress covered with tiny flowers, but she still seemed a little sad. She kept dabbing at her eyes with her handkerchief.

"What are you girls doing here?" she asked as she spotted Nancy and her friends.

"You're not going to believe this . . ." George waved for Mimsy to follow them. "But we found your roses!"

As the band started a lively song, the judges stepped onstage. They were huddled with Helene Flossenhammer, showing her the tallies from their clipboards. "Wait!" Nancy called out to them. "We just need one more minute. There's one late entry! Follow us!"

The judges seemed puzzled. Slowly, they stepped down from the stage and walked after the girls. A small crowd formed around the girls, who were the youngest guests at the gala by at least forty years. Pierre pushed past them to the dessert table, with Jean-Claude trailing behind. "There they are," Pierre said. "Do you think you can still use them?"

"Where?" Bess asked. There were piles of éclairs on silver trays. Dishes of crème brûlée sat out. She could smell the burned sugar on top. But she didn't see the flowers anywhere.

"What happened? What do you mean you found them?" Mimsy asked. She looked worried. "They're not here."

Pierre pointed to the five-tier mousse cake.

There, on the very top of the chocolate frosting, was the cluster of peach roses. They were up so high Nancy hadn't noticed them when she first glanced around the ballroom.

"I can't believe it." George laughed. "We searched everywhere. They were hiding in plain sight."

Mimsy put her hand over her heart. "My little darlings! There they are! And they look just as good as they did this morning!" She grabbed one of the judges' arms and pulled him closer to the dessert table. The man took out his clipboard and wrote down some notes. Soon the other two judges pushed beside him. One stood on a chair to get closer to the blooms.

"They found my roses!" Mimsy called to a few of her friends. Mrs. Canter and Geraldine DeWitt both came over to see. Geraldine didn't look happy. Her red lips were twisted into a sneer.

"With not a minute to spare! What a relief," Helene Flossenhammer said. "How in the world did they get on top of Jean-Claude's cake?"

Nancy and her friends turned to Pierre. His cheeks were bright red. "It was a misunderstanding," Nancy said. The crowd looked confused, but she didn't go on. Even if he'd done something wrong, she didn't want to embarrass him in front of everyone. It was only when Helene finally walked away that Nancy and Pierre explained to Mimsy what happened.

"I'm so sorry," Pierre kept repeating. "I didn't mean to upset you."

Mimsy nodded. "I wish you'd told me the truth sooner. I was so upset. But that said . . . maybe this wouldn't have happened if it wasn't for Jean-Claude."

Jean-Claude straightened up at the mention of his name. "What does this have to do with me?" he asked.

"If you would've been nicer to Pierre, he wouldn't have been afraid to tell you what happened. You can't just yell at everyone all the time." She pointed a finger in Jean-Claude's face. The pastry chef stomped his foot several times.

"I will not explain myself. He is always forgetting what I tell him!" Jean-Claude yelled. Then he huffed off, slamming a side door behind him.

Mimsy just shook her head. She was so excited, nothing could shake her good mood. "I can't thank you enough," she said. She gave Nancy, Bess, and George a big hug. "If it wasn't for you, all my hard work would've been for nothing. You really saved the day."

Nancy smiled. "We're so glad we could help."

"Another case solved," Bess said.

George was still laughing. "I can't believe where we found them!"

She was about to go on, but the band stopped playing. The judges walked back onto the stage. They said something to Helene and she followed them up, grabbing a basket of ribbons from the stairs. She tapped the microphone before speaking into it. "It's now time to announce the winners. First place for the Tulip Garden goes to . . ."

Nancy could barely listen. Helene went through the Tulip Garden winners, the Lilac Garden winners, and the Orchid Garden winners. She called out the winners of five other gardens before she got to the Rose Garden. She'd saved it for last.

Third place went to a woman Nancy hadn't heard of. She climbed the stairs to the stage and took her yellow ribbon. "And second place goes to . . . ," Helene said. "Geraldine DeWitt!"

"Could Miss Bouret have won?" George asked. Geraldine climbed onto the stage. Her face was serious as she took the red ribbon.

The crowd was silent. Nancy squeezed Bess's hand. She was so nervous. It was like she had entered the Garden Show herself. Finally Helene looked back down at the paper in her hands. She took a deep breath. "And first place goes to Mimsy Bouret!"

Nancy cheered. People clapped as Mimsy took

the stage. Helene passed her the blue ribbon. "Thank you," Mimsy said into the microphone. "And thank you, Nancy Drew, Bess Marvin, and George Fayne. I owe it all to you."

Nancy and her friends smiled. It felt good to see Mimsy so happy, and to know that they had helped make her day special. By solving the mystery of the missing roses, the Clue Crew had helped Mimsy finally get the ribbon she deserved.

"I know winning isn't everything," Bess said. "But it sure feels good sometimes."

Nancy watched Mimsy take a bow. She was smiling so much her cheeks hurt. "Definitely," she agreed.

FLOWER POWER

Nancy, Bess, and George spent all day looking at beautiful roses, tulips, and lilies. Now you can turn an ordinary pen into a pretty bloom with these easy steps.

You Will Need:
- Basic blue or black pens, without the caps
- Green floral tape
- Fake flowers

Optional:

- A small terra-cotta planter (no bigger than 6 inches across)
- Paint and paintbrushes
- A cup of small stones (the size of coins)

Directions

- **Step 1:** Choose one flower and one pen.
- **Step 2:** Hold the pen so the tip points down. Place the fake flower against the pen, so the stem runs along its side. (The bloom should hang over the top of the pen.)
- **Step 3:** Using the floral tape, tape the top of the stem to the top of the pen.
- **Step 4:** Wrap the floral tape around the pen from top to bottom. Be sure to cover the flower's stem with the tape.
- **Step 5:** When you reach the bottom of the pen, cut or rip the tape. Secure the end and voilà! You have a beautiful blooming pen.

If you make several pens, you may want to make a "planter" to hold them in. This is the perfect way to create a colorful, fun (and fake) bouquet.

- **Step 1:** Paint your terra-cotta planter with any pattern or design you like.
- **Step 2:** Fill the planter with small stones.
- **Step 3:** "Plant" your flower pens in the pot. They'll be waiting for you the next time you need them.

WHEN YOU'RE A KID, the MYSTERIES ARE JUST that MUCH *BIGGER* ...

NANCY DREW AND THE CLUE CREW
#2
SECRET SAND SLEUTHS

All-new comics from
PAPERCUTZ™!